OLIVIA
Measures Up

adapted by Maggie Testa
based on the screenplay written by Patricia Resnick
illustrated by Jared Osterhold

Ready-to-Read

Simon Spotlight
New York   London   Toronto   Sydney   New Delhi

Based on the TV series OLIVIA™ as seen on Nickelodeon™

SIMON SPOTLIGHT
An imprint of Simon & Schuster Children's Publishing Division
1230 Avenue of the Americas, New York, New York 10020
OLIVIA™ Ian Falconer Ink Unlimited, Inc. and © 2013 Ian Falconer and Classic Media, LLC . All rights reserved.
All rights reserved, including the right of reproduction in whole or in part in any form.
SIMON SPOTLIGHT, READY-TO-READ, and colophon are registered trademarks of Simon & Schuster, Inc.
For information about special discounts for bulk purchases, please contact Simon & Schuster Special Sales at
1-866-506-1949 or business@simonandschuster.com.
Manufactured in the United States of America 1112 LAK
First Edition
1 2 3 4 5 6 7 8 9 10
ISBN 978-1-4424-5973-1 (pbk)
ISBN 978-1-4424-5974-8 (hc)
ISBN 978-1-4424-5980-9 (eBook)

It is a big day for Olivia!
She is finally tall enough
to go on the big-kid rides
at the amusement park!

Ian wants to go
on the big-kid rides too.

But he is not tall enough.

Whee!
Olivia loves the
roller coaster.

After the ride, Father tells
Olivia that Ian will probably
be bigger than her
when they grow up.

Olivia does not like
the sound of that!

At lunchtime Ian wants to
drink some milk.
"That is a good choice,"
says Father.
"Milk will make you tall."

Olivia offers Ian
a glass of water.
"Milk," says Ian.
"How about lemonade?"
Olivia asks.
"Milk," Ian repeats.

Back at home,
Olivia drinks some milk
and calls Julian.

If Ian will not stop growing,
then Olivia will just
grow faster.
"Pull harder," says Olivia.

"If you keep growing,
you will not be able to
ride your bike,"
Olivia tells Ian.

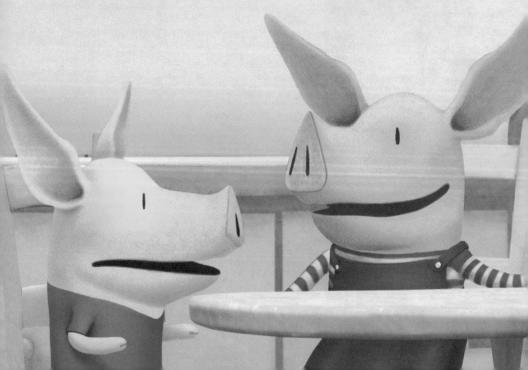

"Or play hide-and-seek,"
adds Julian.
"That sounds terrible,"
says Ian.
"I will try to stop growing."

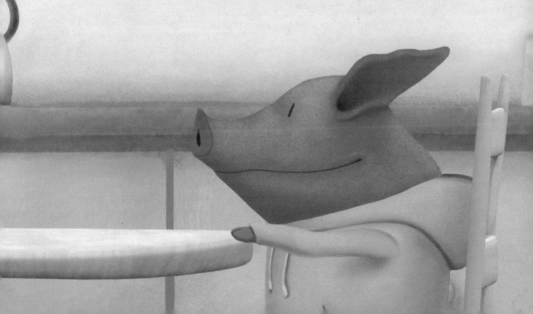

"How tall will I be when I grow up?" Ian asks Father. "You will be about my height," replies Father.

"Can you ride a bike?
Can you play hide-and-seek?"
Ian asks Father.
Father answers yes and yes.

Ian decides that he will grow. "You are making a big mistake," says Olivia.

"Little brothers
should not be taller than
their big sisters!"

The next day is
picture day at school.

Olivia wants to stand
in the back row, but she
is not tall enough.

But that does not stop Olivia!

Smile, everyone!

Before bed Father explains
something to Olivia.
"Even if Ian grows taller,
you will always be
his big sister."